Y

Berenstain
Bear scouts

BeR

copy 2

✓

The Bear Scouts

This title was originally catalogued by the Library of Congress as follows: Berenstain, Stanley. The bear scouts, by Stan and Jan Berenstain. [New York] Beginner Books [1967] 62 p. col. illus. 24 cm. "B-46." I. Berenstain, Janice, joint author. II. Title. PZ10.3.B4522Be 67—21919 ISBN: 0-394-80046-X ISBN: 0-394-90046-4 (lib. bdg.)

The Bear Scouts

by Stan and Jan Berenstain

BEGINNER BOOKS   A Division of Random House, Inc.

Good-bye, Bear Scouts!
Good luck! Have fun!
Isn't Dad going camping
With you, Son?

Not this time.
We don't need Pa.
We've got the Bear Scout
Guidebook, Ma.
It tells us all
We need to know
About camping out
And where to go.

A guidebook, Son?
Now, wait a minute!
I know more
Than the book has in it.

A smart bear opens
His eyes wide
And never needs
A Bear Scout Guide.

Now, Son, stop.
Right here you'll see
Just why you need
A guide like me!

What would you do,
My fine young scout,
To get across
When a bridge is out?

The book says first,

"In such a spot . . .

Tie your rope

With a Bear Scout knot."

Scout knot—bah!

A smart bear knows

He has no need

For one of those.

He ties his *own* knot

To the tree

And safely crosses.

Now watch me.

9

We're here, Scouts.
But Dad is not!
What has happened
To his knot?

On second thought—
I'll stay with you.
So I can show you
What to do.
That camp ground is so far,
You see,
You really need
A guide like me.

Look here, Bear Scouts.
Your book can't show
Which way is
The way to go.
But a bear like me,
A bear who's clever,
Takes the short way.
The long way? Never!

14

But, Papa, wait!
Here's a map in the book.
It says to go
The long way. Look!

Well, you'll find me

At the other end.

A smart bear takes

The short way, friend.

19

On second thought,
I'll come along.
Just in case
Something goes wrong.

21

Now that I've brought you
Safely here,
We'll get down this river.
Never fear.

Yes, Papa. Look.
Here's a plan in the book.

It shows us all
We need to do . . .

To build a fine
Bear Scout canoe.

Build a canoe?
That takes too long!
A bear who's smart
Will know that's wrong.
It's easy to see
That's much too slow.
I know a faster
Way to go.

So long, Bear Scouts!
Toodle-oo!
You can have
Your slow canoe.

I never like
To wait around.
I'll meet you
At the camping ground.

We're coming, Dad!
Just grab the rope.
The Guidebook says
There's always hope.

On second thought—
I'll go with you.
Then I can show you
What to do.
If you go on
And I do not,
You'll never find
Your camping spot.

You won't need
The Guidebook now.
Here's where I really
Show you how.
For this is where
We set up camp,
And I'm the world's
Camp set-up champ!

BEAR SCOUT
CAMPING
GROUND

Now watch this.
I'm really good
At starting a fire
By rubbing wood.

37

Excuse me, Dad.

That way's not right.

The book says

That will take all night.

We'll try this way.
It ought to light.
Look! Now our fire
Is burning bright.

Bear Scouts, you're
Going to have a treat.
I'll cook you something
Good to eat.

A wise bear knows
There's a meal to be found
Wherever he is,
If he just looks around.

I'll put in some eggs
And fresh green weeds.
Some toadstools. Then
Some roots and leaves.
And presto, chango,
Ala kazoo . . .
That's how I make
My favorite stew.

Dad, your stew
Is stewing well.
But doesn't it have
A funny smell?

Besides, the book says,
"For the best camp dish,
Take your rods
And catch some fish."

On second thought—
I'll share your meal.
My stew's a bit
Too rich, I feel.

Now, Scouts, you'll find
A bear who's bright
Will make his bed
While it's still light.

The Guidebook says—
Page eighty-eight—
"Put up your tents
Before it's late."

52

Tents are for sissies!
Be smart, be brave!
You haven't camped out
Till you've slept
in a cave.

Ow! That was quite
A fall I took.
You'd better come
And

BRING

THAT

BOOK!

We're coming, Dad.
No need to worry.
We'll have you mended
In a hurry.

First, bandage nose,
Then thumb, then head.
Then put me
On a rescue sled.

Well done, Bear Scouts!
We're nearly there,
Thanks to your
Smart old Papa Bear.
As I have told you
All along,
With a guide like me,
You can't go wrong.

Dad has shown us
Quite a lot
About what's smart
And what is not.